FEVER
INDUCED

POLISHED PENNY

Table of Contents

CHAPTER ONE

The 93 miles south southeast (SSE) from Key West, Florida to Varadero, Cuba, flies by like a mockingbird painting on her mascara at 105 mph cruise speed. "Que Suerte!" Brass listens to Vivaldi's Spring Violin Concerto No. 1 and conducts with her right pointer finger. Leveling in, like a buzzing queen bee and congregating towards the baptismal river, she lines herself up, single file, and follows in towards the horizon.

Brass bellows out, "Right on time!" She shoots the 6-foot, 1-inch, 233 lbs., blue-eyed, Wailer a dazzling, pearly white smile. Feeling exhilarated, the back of

Brass' thighs, sweaty, stuck to her seat in the cockpit. Her buttocks squeeze tight while she pulls up and bears down on her naval. With a deep release of breath, she grips the metal stick between her thighs and glides in the plane.

The lightly built 1946 Luscombe metal frame, with its fabric, stretched 35-foot wingspan, flocks in. The sun is setting, and Wailer cannot help but exhale. The salty air, the squawks from the rose-throated parrots, and the glowing pink neon horizon help him relax. He rests his clenched fists and sweaty palms on his khaki mountaineering, insect-repellent cargo pants.

Starting to breathe into his inner happy place and watching Brass, he taps his right foot in rhythm with hers. She had a way of soothing him. It was her glow, her steady breath. The more at ease she was, he became at ease. He presses his lips into the mic. "Paradise."

Brass glances at Wailer, leaning her head and bouncy golden curls onto his shoulder. "Close enough."

Batting her brown eyes, she points to her right and mouths, "Rosa."

As a young art student in her early 20s, Brass had started rendezvousing once a month for the National Guard, and thirteen years of training in South Africa and deployments to Afghanistan had made her golden on the stick. After meeting her in Iraq, Wailer encouraged Brass to train in his hometown north of Cape Town. As a former Green Beret and contractor for the Department of State, he had jumped with many pilots, but Brass was different. At the Al Rashid Hotel in Baghdad, Wailer and Brass had partied together.

Brass had asked, "What do you do here in Baghdad?"

"I kill people with my pinky finger," Wailer had whispered with a cocky grin.

The two immediately connected. Wailer believed Brass to be born with feathers. Her keen instincts and ability to read the wind were superhuman at times. He would follow Brass anywhere. He had. Brass and Wailer match amazingly together. Her dynamic aerobatic pilot skills and enhanced training in unusual flight conditions complemented his trained Army Ranger Airborne jumping training. Their attraction to each other and their passion for the air made them both a dynamic and magnetic team. The two now operated a small premiere sky diving club in Key West. The business was booming even with the club being members-only and closed to the public.

Brass gives Wailer a one-minute warning before they reach their target. Holding the package in his lap, he scans below, looking for Rosa. The palace is within sight. Brass shared her excitement to see her sister, Rosa, just hours before on the phone call. Brass knows her sister will be on the rooftop waiting for the flyover.

Feeling shaky and jittery, Rosa rolls her juicy, pink bubble gum around her tongue and looks out the window. Listening to an engine hum overhead, like a dozen violins in unison, Rosa feels nauseous. Her stomach is churning with butterflies. Her hands are clammy, and her heart beats in her chest. Pushing past the dull headache and taking deep breaths, Rosa raises one hand and places it on her heart.

Rosa practices her box breathing: two breaths in and one breath out through the mouth, a skill practiced to calm herself in tense situations. The other hand lays on her stomach. She is biting her lip. Another breath, and she tastes the cherry flavor of her bubble gum mixed with a drop of metallic blood.

Rosa imagines the birds flying and soaring and their wings stretched out. Slowly she blows a bubble with her breath. Pop! Her pulse slows down, and her eyelids weigh heavy as she reaches for the door and walks onto the rooftop. A cool breeze moves over her face like the supple fingertips of her blind grandmother's hands. Anxiety expels out of her mouth with a burp. Rosa stands panting on the roof. Rosa clicks out in thought. Clicking out is when the mind is awake but in a dream-like vision or trance.

"If only I would have had someone to hold my hand," Rosa recalls standing in front of the mirror, huddled in her parents' small trailer bathroom.

Blinking back to reality and wiping a tear away, Rosa focuses again on her breath and listens to the parrots as they circle above the rainforest canopy of trees. The breeze again sweeps over Rosa. The lush green leaves wave to her. Welcome back. The trees beckon her with thousands of emerald eyes looking upon her. They know the island. The trees are like Rosa's mother. They know her. She senses their eyes upon her. Captivated by the pink setting sun, the squalling birds, and the humming of the distant engine in the sky, Rosa recalls laughing in the garden. Far away, laughter, like little girl giggles and the echoes of a brother's voice, resonates in Rosa's ear.

Rosa feels safe, secure, and protected, but he is watching her. There is no pain, no headaches. They play together, brother and sister. He opens the gate for her, and she enters the secret garden. Rosa stares at the enormous tree in the garden's center in awe. He is there. His voice beckoned her to play, to run to dance. She feels how warm he is. She kneels and gazes up at the tree. Warm, strong, and rooted in trust, he wraps his vast forgiving wings around her soft arms. His feathers tickle her skin. Rosa giggles, and he whispers a secret into her ear. "Oh, brother," Rosa's heart quickens as he peers into her eyes and holds her hand. An electric tingle buzzes around Rosa's head.

Brass banks the white tail dragger, hard right. Focusing on the yellow spaghetti straps of Rosa's sun dress, Wailer hurls the premade parachuting black box out the window. He had carefully programmed and packed the equipment and was confident it would provide the intelligence needed. Her eyes gleamed up towards the sky. Rosa traces the package on an invisible wire while beaming up at Wailer. His aim and calculated trajectory nail it to the roof, a reverberating thud. The package smashes onto the pebble-flat rooftop. With a resounding thump, the box crashes at Rosa's feet. With a jolt, Rosa is shocked back again to reality.

Her feet stung as if she had just jumped out of a swing from the elementary school play yard. Feeling sick with nervous energy, the vibrations from the prop plane shot through her body, and adrenaline coursed into her veins. Her mind is swimming. Rosa stares off as her sister Brass flies into the sunset from above. Rosa blinks back more tears, which roll down her soft rose-petal cheeks. There is little time left.

She rips at the bundle with pale knuckles and fights with the packing tape. The strings splice her fingers like tiny paper splinters. Instantly, sucking and biting at the cut like a snake bite, she spits blood and gum onto the rooftop. Untangling strings and tape like a knot of surprise in her gut, she sets up the instruments and directs them to the setting sun. Rosa listens as the tail dagger banks hard left and flies off with the birds.

CHAPTER TWO

Setting up quickly, Rosa aims for the solar panels to align with the setting sun. Viewing the sun, she rapidly installs the unit. With her watch, she manipulates a few frequencies and adjusts several channels. The instrument is downloading. Engrossed, jaw slightly dropped, Rosa snips screenshots. Before her gleaming green eyes, the numbers puzzle her.

Moving stealthily, she makes her way back down the split staircase. Within minutes the thumb drive is back in the heart of the cold marble-carved desk.

Taking in one more breath, Rosa looks up at the dome ceiling above her. In awe, she sighs.

The original owner, an executive with the Chesapeake and Ohio Railroad Company, built the marble palace in 1912. The Italianate marble villa, with 52 rooms, was built as a token of love for his darling wife, May. When they were not in Cuba, the husband and wife resided in Richmond, back in the States. The palace had changed hands, and the new family shared a kindred spirit with Rosa.

The castle was Rosa's favorite place to work. It felt like home to her: warm, welcoming, and grand. She sensed she had been here before, moreover, long before she started cleaning the palace. Bricked walk-ways outside led to more marble steps and hidden trails. Stables and a magnificent ecclesiastical watch-tower guarded the sacred and secret gardens. Built-up marble walls contained gardens and overflowing white Butterfly Jasmine. The scent often hypnotized

Rosa, and she found herself lingering after work, walking in meditation, praying, and chanting melodies like a soft dove cooing at dusk. Sculptures of cherubim angels stand guard within fountains of water. They were dotting the fancy corners of the grounds. A quaint-looking glass reflection pond mirrors the palace up to the heavens. Oh, it was grand indeed.

For a moment, time stops. Rosa only hears her heartbeat and recalls the story of the two Olympian gods: Poseidon, the God of the seas, and Athena, the goddess of wisdom and skill. Gathering up her cleaning supplies and Kenmore vacuum, Rosa looks at the 4,000-piece Tiffany stained-glass window bearing the likeness of Athena.

Rosa leaps into her candy-red Jeep and pulls off towards the runway. Her emerald eyes bounce in her rear-view mirror; she fires a menthol Virginia Slim cigarette. Her nerves are grasping for anything to hold on to. Cleaning at the palace over the last several months had been different. Something wasn't feeling right. Something was bothering her.

Rosa started cleaning residential homes on the island within weeks of first arriving. The headaches were an everyday reminder of what she had left behind—a dull pain of heartache. She dared to hope that the island would help her and heal her.

Since the entire island is slightly smaller than the state of Pennsylvania, Rosa became very attuned to her surroundings. Her polite English and Spanish language increased her success in making friendships. It has always been a gift that she holds dearly. Her fantastic ability to communicate, read people, and listen throws her into a very elite group of clients.

Mostly cleaning vacation homes for ambassadors and senators, Rosa makes it a rule to keep busy and deaf. "When Sense Matters, Call Polished Pennies." Most clients only know her as Penny. Very few, if any, know her real name. Rosa had come to the island for a sabbatical, and the church nuns had helped her keep the hope alive. Since 1702, the Discalced Carmelites graced the streets and ministered to the hungry and diseased. The sisters dealt a lot with cholera. The polished petite 5' 5" brunette that weighs in at about a buck fifty – five often hides among the corridors and hidden pathways of the convent. Rosa was not one to wander into the streets when the sisters made their rounds to visit the sick. They whisper about her in hushed tones. Cleaning provided a way for Rosa to venture out and feel protected within the walls of the many homes and gardens she kept.

CHAPTER THREE

Over a drink at the local banana rum pub, Brass and Wailer view the screenshots from Rosa's camera.

"I know a contact near Guantanamo," Rosa whispers to her sister. "He's a friend of a friend and may be able to help decipher the encrypted bearings."

"I've already contacted someone," announces the broad-shouldered Wailer. "We used to work detail together in the Middle East. His ETA is 19 hundred." Rosa's sun-kissed bare legs turn to the rhythm of the Cuban drums. Rocking her hips, Rosa beckons

Wailer with her sparkling eyes. In a trance, Wailer moves toward Rosa. Whispering in his left ear and pulling him close to salsa dance, Rosa says, "Maybe we will find some treasure, eh!" Smiling into her gaze, Wailer hopes that is all they find. Knowing the source, and the drop off of the solar equipment, Wailer is glad that he called Crawl for backup.

Crawl takes a deep breath and rolls his shoulders down as he enters the pub. Wailer breaks away from the dance as soon as the song ends, and there is a change in tempo. Crawl and Wailer shake hands and hug. Rosa rejoins her sister at the table. The girls wink and giggle at each other with nervous energy. They embrace over laughs and rum.

"What is someone like you doing with this kind of information?" Crawl eyes Rosa up and down. To Crawl, Rosa appears bewildered. Crawl thinks of her and has trepidation, but simultaneously, he knows Rosa—her strength and excitement. As soon as Crawl entered the bar, Crawl connected with her. He started thinking of her before he arrived. Sitting beside Rosa, Crawl leans in close to talk with her. Like a magic spell, Rosa is mesmerized by Crawl's ocean-blue eyes. Everyone at the pub fades into the background.

Crawl has just returned from Egypt. It was a research expedition. He shares with Rosa about past lives and reads Akashic records. Rosa watches his soft lips and wonders what they taste like. She wants to run her fingers through his sandy brown hair and lightly touch his muscular arms to persuade him closer. Rosa can feel his energy as he talks and senses her body coming to life like a spark of fire inside her. Breathing in and out of her mouth, she feels his energy. His light is radiating.

Mentally Rosa starts stripping off her clothes and her mortal body. Lulled by her breath, Rosa starts to entwine with Crawl on a deep energy level, almost out of this world. It must be the sound of his voice.

It sounds so familiar, strong, and full of trust. Crawl explains the pyramids. How thoughts, words, emotions, and intent occur in the past, present, and future. "I know you." Crawl looks into Rosa's eyes. "And not just now. I have known you from before." Crawl declares to Rosa as if declaring his love. "We planned this, Rosa. We planned to meet right here and tonight in this pub long before. Ages ago in the Ancient of days." Rosa starts to cry. She cannot help it. All the emotions from the day. All the feelings are bursting up through her, and now this. Is Crawl confessing his love to her within minutes of the meeting? Or has it been minutes? What were these Akashic records? Had they met before? Had they planned this? It's too much for Rosa. She excuses herself to the restroom.

Looking into the mirror, Rosa stares into the mirror, splashing her face with cold water and sighing. Leaving to go back out to meet with Crawl and the others, she bumps into a sweet little grandmother entering the restroom.

"Bueno hija." The grandmotherly woman looks up at Rosa. The older woman with eyes brown and full like sweet-baked chocolate chips smile at Rosa. "You look familiar to me. Have we met?" asks Rosa.

Rosa introduces herself in her best Spanish.

The grandmother holds out a cup of tea for Rosa. She proclaims, "Tears cut stone."

Rosa only briefly registers the message; however, she does know enough about body language to realize that this sweet grandmother is a medicine woman offering her something to soothe her soul and stomach. The nuns and sisters had taught Rosa about the medicine women when she went to market. Rosa listened intently to these women. The sisters shared how they would bring unique, magical, and holy water from off the mountains and give it to the children to drink and to the mothers to aid them in healing their children from diarrhea. The medicine women often painted their hands, fingers, and feet with exotic symbols and markings.

With a slurp and a gulp, a puckered face, Rosa downs the tea. There is no time for sipping. The medicine woman places her hands on Rosa's heart. A warm wave flows over Rosa—the light flickers. There must be lightning nearby. Rosa has noticed the high occurrences of power surges while on the island. The lights flicker again. The grandmother is gone.

"Here she comes." Wailer's eyes signal to Crawl.

"Hello." Rosa softly sits back down beside Crawl, almost floating on air. The tea has her whole-body tingling. Taking Crawl's arm, she holds it firmly. Feeling his tight bicep muscle, she starts to melt again. Crawl looks into Rosa's eyes. "This is a bit too much for me. I feel flattered and overwhelmed." Rosa barely gets her words out while tears well up in her eyes like fresh pools of water. She reaches now for Crawl's hand.

"I know." Tears well up in his eyes; Rosa yearns, "Could it be these two hearts?"

Instinctively, Crawl agrees to help Rosa and her friends get to the island's south shore. In hushed tones, Crawl leans in and slides his iPhone across the bar out of range; Crawl knows of agencies like NSA that can access your devices through in-built back-doors. He had even worked on an Extortion Mission, and his team could tune in on their target phone's microphone.

"These are grid coordinates, and they are within protected waters." The GIS satellite images of these perimeters are secret only.

Crawl is familiar with reading radar remote sensing technology as he worked for a contractor that created mapping images. Although he is in early retirement and swearing to himself that he would never again get involved with treasure-hunting expeditions, he doesn't even try to resist Rosa. Reading her body language, he senses her unease and leans forward and expounds. "Mostly only scientists who study imaginary phenomena are granted permissions for research with the public affairs department to enter these waters." Intrigued by Rosa, Crawl agrees to lead the team into the water.

Up for an adventure and captivated by his sweet spirit sister, Crawl packs his boat and is ready. Dear spirit, sister. He read stories of this type of woman. Only in his wildest dreams did he think he would have a soulmate. The four enter the boat. Crawl follows the curves of the water coves and speeds towards the bay. The night is thick and sticky. He taps on the barometer, questioning if his instruments are working.

The yellow glow of the crocodile's eyes keeps Crawl on high alert. An expert on tracking and studying alligators and Cuban Crocodiles, Crawl slows his speed before entering the open waters. Tour guiding is his new sport, and it's even led him to Egypt to study the sacred animal. Written evidence for Croc keepers is scarce. Egyptians emphasized the care of their Crocs. Supposedly they were captured and bred by the thousands. Worshipers bought baby crocodiles, sacrificed them, and mummified them. The vows of the Egyptians intrigued Crawl.

Along with the Crocs was the study of their feathered friend and the cult of the hawk (sacred to Horus). Crawl going to Egypt was like a needle in a compass aligning to its true north. Crawl stares at Rosa out of the corner of his eye. She feels like Egypt to him, a missing key to a map.

Crawl has learned to stay in the boat and protect himself from the wildlife. Like a Toyota Prius, he silently stalks the edge of the rim of the reef.

Eyeing Rosa's beautiful, soft figure, he switches to electric power and kills the gasoline engine.

Brass's thin white, cotton top breathes more unrestricted in the open air with the moonlight high in the sky.

"Thank you for flying in, Sis." Rosa looks up to Brass. "I have a great feeling about this adventure!"

"Anytime," says Brass. "It was a bit of a push to make it here before sunset. What was the rush?"

Rosa tunes out the questions coming from her sister. She is starting to doubt all the information, dreams, and tears.

"Up ahead is the unspoiled reef." Crawl points. "Los Jardines de La Reina. Named the Queen's Garden, American scientists face delays due to political strains between Washington and Havana, but we all know that is lifting now."

Happy for a distraction, Rosa leans in to hear more of what Crawl is saying. It's not that Rosa doesn't want to share with her sister. It's just that Rosa herself doesn't understand the dreams completely, but she knows that the numbers have pulled her in like some portal spinning in her sleep.

CHAPTER FOUR

At 1,200 feet from the point, Crawl shuts down the electric power. Surveying the water, he snarls, "The wind is up, and so is the current." He taps more on his instruments. "Do you see that glow?" Wailer shouts above the wind. "It's just below the waves. Is that the reflection of the moon or something glowing in the water?" Wailer heightens his awareness, adrenaline pulses through his blue veins. Then there is a strong gust of wind. It feels close to 34 mph.

Crawl searches his navigations. The Beaufort is reading eight. Too high for a clear night. The

Beaufort scale is an empirical measure that relates to wind speed. The gust picks up frothy waves and smacks them into the sides of the converted lobster boat.

Unsteadily, Rosa falls into the back of the boat.

"Rosa, give me your hand." Stammering, Crawl locks eyes. He again feels her magnetic pull. Befuddled, he lunges from the control towards her and stretches out his right hand. Feeling heat like fire within the palm of Rosa's hand, Crawl tries to pull her forward, but from the left, a dark shadowy wet mass swipes her. Another round of turbulent waves swells around the tiny vessel. Within seconds, water is aboard.

Rosa falls into the salty, crocodile-filled bay. The wind, the current, the light, the necessity for silence amid the rage, and the confusion angers Crawl. Crawl throws himself toward the edge. Dismayed, searching the water in milliseconds, he glimpses a glow and steadies himself to dive.

"No!" Wailer shouts as he throws life jackets into the dark waters.

The metal boat churns in circles like a meat grinder. The waves once again unlock Crawl's grasp. Knowing he must think quickly to save the other two souls on board, Crawl commands, "Hold on!" The aerated water feels like a black hole sucking them in. The vessel needed to be more buoyant. It was much more challenging to stay afloat. Shifting all the weight to the left and shouting like guiding a raft down a class five rapid, Crawl keeps the boat from capsizing.

The boat spins counterclockwise as it floats on top of water bubbles exploding with the sound of firecrackers. Crawl studies the water. It's as if it is boiling. The water splashing into the boat is almost colder than the salty air around him.

With a jolting thud, the boat hits the edge of the island. Brass and Wailer watch Crawl. His lips move, but they cannot hear what he says. Everything is happening within milliseconds. His words are only coming through in waves. Wailer feels a little sick.

Crawls explains his thoughts methodically to Wailer and Brass as if repeating information out loud while taking notes in a chemistry class at Stanford Research Institute (SRI). Crawl took a summer semester at SRI in California before joining the military as an officer.

"Cavitation, it's a phenomenon." Says Crawl.

"It happens when the atmospheric pressure drops. As pressure drops, bubbles start forming in the water, and the water starts to boil. The bubbles imploding are full of steam vapor. The boiling sea water produces vapor, and when these bubbles pop, they make much noise. A few scientists know that if you reduce atmospheric pressures, water will boil at lower temperatures."

Crawl scans his instruments and reads the pressure per square inch. He knows he should have a reading of 14.70 psi. To his astonishment, the barometric pressure is reading at almost zero psi. The water temperature is 68 degrees Fahrenheit, 20 degrees Celsius. Cavitation must be why the scientist comes here to study the phenomenon at the reef, he thinks to himself, but he doesn't have the energy to share any more with his comrades.

"Can you stand up?" asks Crawl to Wailer. "Good, we must keep going. Come on; it's time to go."

Climbing out of the boat and scratching his head, Crawl looks into the water. They had only been about 34 yards from the island when the phenomenon occurred. "Rosa must have swum to shore; she must be on the shore." Crawl tries to hold back tears, but his chin quivers.

Wailer, carrying Brass over his shoulder, makes it into the jungle. "Look at me," says Wailer as he holds up Brass's tearful face in the palms of his hands. "Trust me," he says, "I don't know what the hell that was, but there is something in the water. I saw it. I caught a fleeting glimpse out of the corner of my eye. I turned to look, but Rosa was gone. It would be best if you trusted me. Do you trust me?"

Brass stares up into his blue eyes, but Wailer knows Brass is entirely numb, unable to process the loss, the confusion, the antagonism. Blinking, "I feel it." Brass cries. "I mean, I felt it. Out there, out in the water. I felt the pull right before the wave came down on Rosa." Just then, another burst of light comes from under the water out in the bay.

"We need to get going," coughs Crawl. "We are not the only ones seeing and hearing all this."

"He's right," Wailer says. Reaching out his hand toward Brass, "We must keep moving." They feel the ground rumble and shake beneath them.

Knowing that her sister is an excellent swimmer, Brass envisions Rosa is somehow alive, but they must find her within the next 72 hours, or else someone else will. Brass grabs Wailer's hand. She whispers into his ear, "I trust you."

Following the blue light of the global positioning system, Crawl leads the three to a boulder or outcrop of rocks. Pulling back thick vines, Crawls stares at the monoliths. Everyone takes a step back. Crawl brushes the sand and dirt off the engravings. Next, he pours water from his canteen to clean the surface. Brass rummages through her fanny pack and pulls out a bottle of vitamin E oil. Both Crawl and Wailer look at her with curiosity.

"Okay, Mary Poppins, what else is in your carpet bag?" Crawl shakes his head.

Pouring the oil on the stones, Brass reads the rocks like a blind person reading Braille. Brass glances at the fellas and gives them both the "Shhh, my blind grandmother raised me, teaching me to read with my fingertips and eyes." Feeling her way across the stones, she stops. One of the stones is out of place. Brass gently turns the stone 180 degrees. Abracadabra, the stone wall rolls back, and a dark opening appears. The gentlemen turn and look at Brass with disbelief.

"How did you know what to do?" Wailer stumbles back. "You never cease to amaze me." He says to Brass. Picking her up and holding her close to him, he spins her around and kisses her forehead. Slowly lowering her, Brass' feet land on the dirt ground. Falling forward, she leans in and places her head on his shoulder between his collarbone and under his chin. Wailer breathes in. He was thinking to himself, Heaven.

Grounding her balance, Brass wrinkles her nose and replies to Wailer, " You know it's magic." But deep inside her heart, she feels Rosa, and her thoughts quickly fade. She had a way of connecting with Rosa like this. It started when the kidnapping happened when Rosa was only three and Brass was five. Their

Father took the sisters from their mother. The kidnapping bonded the two sisters with a deep entanglement and a wicked sick sense while they were gone. All they had was each other during these months. Brass remembers the games they would play. The hide and seek. They always promised to find each other.

Crawl can barely swallow looking into Brass's deep, soft brown eyes. "This way," he manages to summon the words.

Time seems to stop, but Crawl's legs keep moving. "How could I have lost my grip? What if sharks have eaten her? No, no. Maybe she is okay; maybe she made it to shore. We were so close to the shore. She could have swum; she could have floated. She has to be okay." Grabbing his forehead, he feels the blood pulsate through his temples. "What was that? Was it an underwater whirlpool, a vortex in the bay?" The questions in his head have no logical answers. Crawl marches forward, listening to the beat of his pounding heart in his ears—time lapses in the cave tunnel.

CHAPTER FIVE

eing in deep water was not an unfamiliar sensation, having trained herself to be trapped underwater in a white-water kayaking rescue class. Knowing her buoyancy, Rosa instinctively takes herself mentally to her happy place. "One must relax, slow down the heartbeat and wait for rescue." She repeats to herself.

"No, no, no, calvary is coming to save me. The bay is not a flat-water rescue course to help me overcome my fear of water; no, this is real." Feeling desperate, Rosa starts to sink. Swimming vigorously, it feels so challenging to tread this water. She knows she must save herself. The boat disappearing is only an illusion. Being alone in this water is all part of the plan.

"Yes, I planned this. It's a game. Get deeper into the fear. Get deeper, and it will break." Rosa paddles towards the light, the moonlight—discombobulated and disoriented. Rosa swims.

Weeks and weeks of lap swimming year after year at the local YMCA give Rosa an edge in the cool water. She paddles around and searches for the boat. The glow is gone. The current is still. The suction from the eddy leaves her panting for air. She does not know how she escaped that; the wind has died.

"How much time could I have been under the water?" Rosa's thoughts slush behind her eyes. She clings tight to the life-saver jacket with a bear hug. Glancing at her watch, she stammers,

"It only seemed like seconds. Where is the boat?" Her thoughts race in her head, and then she realizes it.

Panicking, she begins to cry and shout, "Help!" Her breath is shallow and quick. Too quick. She starts to hyperventilate. In seconds, the grip of fear, fear for her life, sends a wave of shock into her veins. It would take the strength of an Olympian to remain afloat in this abyss of water. Head above water, Rosa has a flashback and clicks out.

"Rosa, this is called Past Life Regression Work, and we will guide you through it. When you face your fear in the past, it sets you free to live a fuller life now with less fear of dying. The past life meditations will also help you with the trauma, Rosa." Rosa trusts the staff at the institute. They specialize in working with the military and PTSD. Although Rosa is not in the military, her childhood trauma had her in and out of counselors' offices since she was 13. At least, that is when Rosa first really started to feel her energy. A 13-year-old wants life to be every day. To be like all the other girls in school. Rosa repressed her abilities. She hid them under the covers.

The dreams reoccurred. Rosa downplayed them. Who would ever talk to her about them: she journaled, prayed, and dismissed—one day, decades later, all that changed when she met Peaches.

"Rosa, I have an aunt that can help you with your dreams."

"What do you mean?"

"She works at this place that helps people like you."

"What does she do?" Rosa's eyes lift toward Peaches.

"I'm not sure, but I know people keep coming back to see her."

"What is her name?" Rosa searches her purse for a pen.

"Her name is Anne." Peaches squeezes Rosa's hand. With soft eyes and a Southern hug, Peaches gives Rosa the wink, and Rosa is out the door. That's what sisters do. They look out for each other. Peaches is a housekeeper at the institute, and Rosa is a housekeeper in town; they would meet on Mondays. That was their girl day. Sit around the table, read the tabloids - and the National Enquirer.

Laying on the waterbed, the lab technician finishes connecting and taping the monitor wires to Rosa's fingertips. Rosa, now a young woman in her prime, feels ready for answers. She is tired of repressing and not knowing who she is.

"Rosa, you can hear my voice, and I want you to tell me what you see. This may come to you like a dream," instructs Anne, the institute's best lab tech. "We call this mind awake body asleep. First, we will do a relaxation meditation and then count backward until we leave local time. I will guide you and be with you. Remember, Rosa; this is only a simulation."

Rosa sucks on a Tums and takes deep breaths through her mouth. "Okay, Anne, I am ready."

Science was there. Something called Quantum Tunneling. She had seen movies from Hollywood. Something in her resonated with the idea of time travel—the phenomenon of quantum entanglement. The lab tech walked Rosa through the brainwaves again: There will be Delta, Theta, Alpha, Beta, and Gamma. The goal is to relax and have fun. Rosa prayed deep within herself that this experiment would guide her to heal. Guide her to transform the trauma.

Flashing back, "I am in a submarine. It's not good. We are hit. I am helping the doctor, and we are in the middle of surgery." Rosa's eyes dash back and forth as if she were in REM sleep, but her mind is awake, her body asleep.

"What do you see around you, Rosa?" asks Anne.

"I can see Russian symbols. I must be Russian. There is blood, lots of blood. We cannot save this man. We are preparing to surface. I am moving away from the doctor; I must get near the hatch. I must save myself. There are others, but they are wounded. Water is coming in too fast. The vessel is rising to the surface. I can feel it. There is a light flashing. I feel scared and panicked, but I feel numb. I must get to the hatch." Rosa's heart rate is increasing. The lab tech must talk her down. "Rosa, I am with you. Do you see a lifesaver, a life jacket?" whispers the lab tech.

"Yes," says Rosa. Rosa grabs the jacket. There is yelling and men behind her fighting. She focuses on the flashing light of the exit signs—the vessel surfaces. Rosa can sense it. The hatch opens. More men are fighting. Rosa squeezes through and between the men and climbs the ladder to the open air. Another explosion and another torpedo hit the submarine. Rosa is thrown from the hatch exit and into the cold sea. Rosa clutches her life jacket and watches the ship and crew sink back into the water. Swimming not to get sucked down with the boat, she paddles and paddles. Turning around, Rosa is alone in the deep ocean. All alone.

Anne calls out to Rosa, "Are you okay?"

Rosa replies, "I cannot die like that. I cannot face this fear of dying."

"It's okay, Rosa, you did a terrific job. You may have some survivor's guilt, but you faced many fears just now. I am proud of you. I am coming in to check on you now."

The mentoring and meditating work with Anne at the institute cracked the door of possibilities for Rosa. There was no turning back now.

CHAPTER SIX

ith a gasp of air, Rosa choked and coughed up seawater. Rosa wishes she were back in the lab, back in the States, back hidden underground in the remote Blue Ridge Mountains of Virginia with Anne, but she isn't. She is in the sunken Garden of the Queen. Rosa shakes her head. "This is not supposed to be happening. No, I will not die like this. No, I am not ready to die."

Treading the dark ocean water alone, Rosa rises to fill her lungs with air. At the same time, as if able to smell her fear, two sea eels encircle and intertwine around

Rosa's ankles like snakes. Crying out, Rosa feels an electric shock, and her calf muscles contract.

Her legs smack against the sharp coral-like tiny shark teeth bites; the coral cuts into her soft, olive-tanned thighs. Rosa starts a trail of blood.

Like lights along a runway strip, the coral beneath Rosa begins to glow and illuminate beneath her as if lighting her way. Grabbing the edge of a large piece of coral, Rosa fights against the strength of the eels. As her hands grip the edge of the rock, a gigantic coral chunk breaks off; it shimmers and glows before her. She falls into a sinkhole beneath the royal coral garden in the blink of an eye—the black rock bottom seabed breaks from under her. Slipping through a crack, Rosa is now in a cavern.

The ocean floor rumbles with thunder like an earthquake. Rosa's golden-brown hair catches in between the rocks. She dangles like a chandelier in the belly of a vast underwater sea cave. The eels needed to be more maleficent. They dance and joke about each other as if they can speak humanly. Rosa shakes her head in disbelief but is still tangled, her hair caught between the rocks. The eels swim under Rosa. With what looks like a wink and even a grin from them, the eels swim away.

There is no turning back now; Rosa knows this. As if crossing a threshold into the complete and utter unknown, Rosa questions if she is alive or has just experienced her death.

Thank God the cave is full of air, and she is out of the water, but Rosa still repeats her training from the white-water rescue course. In complete darkness, she knows she must react, but slowly. Slow is smooth. Smooth is fast. Rosa knows she must slow her breathing. She must slow everything down. She feels the cuts on her thighs down her leg, inching her fingers. They sting like Mississippi fire ant bites. Rosa continues to box breath in through her mouth and out through her mouth. Finally, she reaches for her knife from around her ankle; Rosa cuts her hair free, falling into the pit.

Covered in vines, Rosa climbs the sides of the crater-shaped hole. Water is flowing in and out with the tide beneath her. Rosa is so puzzled by the karst topography. The cave shimmers with veins of gold. Rosa reads the walls with her hands. She senses the rocks have more sinkholes and sinking streams. Between twigs, pristine crystals and stalactites provide an anchor for her footing. She doesn't understand how to see in this darkness, but the rocks before her have a massive glow as if they are somehow alive.

Mesmerized, Rosa watches as she holds the glowing rocks in her hands. The luminous stones banish the darkness within the pit; she spots a tunnel. Although alone, humming in her ears, her pulse beats with a positive vibration. The vibration is at a low-frequency hertz. She recalls the same beats the institute gave

Rosa to listen to before her meditations. It feels like the delta down here, like a dream. It's not that she hears the frequencies, however. Rosa feels the vibrations like the beat of a drum.

Rosa follows her bearings and listens by using constant humming as a guideline, like a magnetic needle in a compass. Running her hands along the cool limestone walls of the tunnel, she gains speed. The smooth cuts of the corridor switch back and forth like the serpentine walls that Thomas Jefferson built back in Virginia. But these seem much older, more like pre-Toltec aqueduct mazes. The Toltecs were scientists and artists who formed a society of masters (naguals) at Teotihuacan, the ancient city of pyramids outside Mexico City, known as where "Man Becomes God."

Rosa gains and loses elevation like a sound wave traveling through time and space. Like the feathered, plumed serpent of the Mayas and Quiches of Central

America, Gucumatz flashes in Rosa's mind's eye. She can see the snake. Her hideous white fangs ooze with the medicine of death. Breathing again, box breathing again, Rosa embraces the snake's magic and medicine. Feeling her way into the darkness and deafening to her ears, the silence penetrates Rosa. She stops. "Am I imagining this?" Allowing the sensations to take over. "I feel like a snake. I am the snake. I am the medicine. I am Gucumatz." Rosa squeezes between two rocks, feeling completely hypnotized as if drugged by a jungle tea. Rosa remembers the sweet medicine woman.

Opening before her, Rosa gazes at what appears to be a gallery of cave paintings and markings of what looks like Egyptian hieroglyphs. Above Rosa, hoovers, no floats, no hangs, a massive body of water.

Baffled, amazed, and fearful, she falls to the sandy floor. Rosa feels God. She senses her initiation like a priestess who has found her temple. Rosa feels safe.

For some reason, she knows she has been here before. She stands slowly, ever so slowly. Her eyes search the walls for a sign, a location, for a beacon. The paintings depict a path, moving like a sound wave, a snake. Markings, solid and broken lines like an equation, engulf her under the dome of the hanging waters. Paintings of birds appear on the wall and suggest that the path is moving, PULSATING, flying through time, a fabric. The illustrations show human beings moving up the trail into the waters above.

Rosa speaks out into the silent air. As if reading a quantum physics formula, she gets it. "The numbers, the coordinates, the grid, it's a range, a field, an energy vortex." A quantum field.

"Hello?"

The paintings display a maze, like a wellspring of water to the entire world. There are twelve gates and twelve tunnels for the water to flow through. An Atlas is before her.

There is more. Somehow Rosa knows the meaning of the symbols, but Rosa realizes she is not alone. "Hello, who is there?"

"It is I, Gabriel." Rosa is not afraid. The magnificent archangel glows in the light before her eyes. She can hear children laughing as if recalling when she first met Gabriel in the garden back home.

"Gabriel," she whispers. "What am I to do now?"

"Read the stones, Rosa. I am here with you."

Rosa feels safe. She feels the call to do this work. Rosa pulls the vines from a giant monolith in the center of the cave room. Splashing water on the stone, she peers at the unclear images. "I cannot read them," Rosa stammers.

Gabriel asks Rosa to come closer, and he begins pouring oil onto the crown of her head, anointing her. The oil drips down her face and arms and covers her hands. "Now read the stones," declares Gabriel.

Rosa places her hands, covered in oil, on the stones. As if becoming one with the rocks, reading them like her great-grandmother read Braille with her supple fingertips, Rosa also reads the vibrations of the rocks. Rosa starts to decrypt the encrypted codes. A sun, a moon, and many stars. Paintings all around Rosa.

"These etchings are chemical compositions."

"Yes, go on," says Gabriel.

"They are chemistry lessons, like medical prescriptions."

"Yes," says Gabriel. You are passing the test."

"The decryption for sun is vitamin D. The moon equals Calcium. The stars are for Melatonin." Rosa stops. "These are simple and easy vitamins to remember. Hidden in these hieroglyphs are medicines to heal the people."

Rosa feels light coming from Gabriel. It feels like powerful radiation, almost too much to bear.

"Will you trust me?" He speaks to her, and his wings expand and open extensively.

"Of course, yes," Rosa replies as she is yet terrified and in awe. She knows him already, somehow, from somewhere. "We played together before. In the secret garden, the Garden of Eden. I remember playing with you when I was a child."

"Yes, Rosa. Gabriel gently confirms what Rosa is recalling. We played in the garden of your original parents, Father Time and Mother Earth."

Rosa kneels to the ground, taking her small hand in his sweaty grip. There is a hieroglyph of the Tree of Life, and in the middle of the Tree of Life, there is the All-Seeing Eye.

The energy surge coming from Gabriel flows through Rosa's body. "Declare yourself," Gabriel commands Rosa.

"Repeat after me: I love myself unconditionally." Rosa breathes out the words, "I love myself unconditionally."

"Louder," commands Gabriel. "I love myself unconditionally."

"Louder" – "I love myself unconditionally!"

Rosa's hand is locked in his grip. Gabriel orders, "LOUDER!"

She bellows with the deepest breath from the bottom of Rosa's belly. "I LOVE MYSELF UNCONDITIONALLY." The vibrations resonate with the leaves on the tree painting in such a way as a voice's pitch-breaking glass. Rosa breaks the picture of the leaves of the Tree of Life mural. An opening appears, and Rosa's wings burst from her back like a butterfly breaking free of the dead weight of a caterpillar. A black carcass of bloody slime falls off Rosa's branches, and screams of demons vacuum into the cracked walls of the cave. "Gabriel, what was that?" Rosa asks as she looks bewildered at her massive new set of wings.

"Shame," declares Gabriel. "Shame and toxins from your environment."

"Follow me, Rosa, and we will visit our favorite place. You have passed the second phase of your initiations."

"I cannot feel my left leg." Rosa turns to Gabriel. "It's like electricity. Do you feel it, too? It's all through me. I feel paralyzed." With a trigger of fear, Rosa flashes back to her training with Anne.

"Now, when you go out of the body, Rosa, and you want to return, focus on your big toe." Anne raises her eyebrows at Rosa. "You got that? Don't try to get back into your body all at once. It can shock your system. Rather wiggle your big toe."

Taking in as many mental notes as possible, Rosa repeats to herself: "Toes, feet, tapping. There is No Place like Home. I got it, Anne."

After a few minutes, Rosa starts to regain feeling in her leg. Slowly she takes Gabriel's arm and is up on her feet. Her wings are fluffy and silvery white. Holding onto Gabriel's hand, Rosa enters the tree. Turning her head over her shoulder and looking back, she hears jazz music. Vultures are dancing around her old dead carcass. Rosa joins the Tree of Life, the All-Seeing Eye. She knows the All-Seeing Eye and the Tree of Life are the same. One is Egyptian, and the other is Kabbalist. Gabriel takes Rosa deeper into the tree.

Rosa ponders, "It must have been the stories and the training that my great uncle gave me when I was a little girl, maybe when I was five years old."

CHAPTER SEVEN

osa flashes back to her memory bank. "Now look, Rosa, I have to go and clean the lodge today," says her great-uncle, Winston. "I am going to take you with me, but this has to be a secret."

"Okay," Rosa says. She loves to be with her great-uncle. He is her protector, her knight. As soon as Rosa had been found and returned to her mother as a little girl, Winston was a second guardian over her.

The kidnapping by Rosa's Father seemed like a game to her. The memories of what happened were scattered. The psychologist had told Rosa's mother that Rosa likely had to cope and develop different parts of her brain to survive the kidnapping. Rosa was the youngest of all the sisters, remembered the least, or compartmentalized the best.

Great Uncle Winston kept a close watch on Rosa after the kidnapping, rescuing, and returning home to be with her mother and sister, Brass. "I've got my eye on you, kid." He would say to Rosa with a wink. And on that day, he took her to a secret room. However, on this day, there were no doctors or therapists. It was only her and her best pal in the world, Winston.

The checkered floors hypnotized Rosa. Large tapestries decorated the hall with stories, from the heights of the ceilings to the baseboards. "Now, you stay here," said Winston. "I have some business to take care of in the office, and then I need to clean up a little bit."

Rosa walked over to the carved wooden chairs that lined the walls. The chairs have intricate carvings with the claws of lions and the faces of animals. She stared up at the flags and swords. The vibrant colors in the wall hangings mesmerized her. The hourglass full of sand placed on the wooden table kept her attention. A glass case with an old book was in the middle of the room. Rosa gazed into the labyrinth of words.

Uncle Winston came back into the grand room. He sat Rosa on a throne and spoke of the East and the West. Winston talked about the morals, levels, ranks, and degrees of the Masonic Lodge. Rosa learned new words like unanimous and blackball. Rosa first learned of the All-Seeing Eye, the all-pervading intelligence, and the Tree of Life in the secret lodge. Over the next few years, Winston would sneak Rosa into the grand hall every chance he got. Rosa would have a lesson at least once a month.

CHAPTER EIGHT

Like a mother's womb, it is dark in the Tree of Life: soft, warm, and pitch black. There is a seed, however. Like the guiding voice of Anne back at the institute, Gabriel speaks to Rosa. "Touch the seed now, Rosa." Rosa touches the seed pod, and it pricks her finger. Rosa's blood is the key and unlocks the seed pod. Ancient scrolls unwind all around her. Rosa's blood drips onto the parchment paper, and a blueprint, a map, races across the never-ending scrolls like a never-ending story.

"Gabriel, what is this?" Rosa stammers. "This is the DNA of humanity, the Akashic records." He speaks.

"Take a closer look, Rosa," Gabriel commands. Inside the Tree of Life, inside the All-Seeing Eye, Rosa reads the story of life, the records of TIME.

In a heartbeat, Rosa is swimming in the blood. "Impossible," she thinks, but at the same time, Rosa is no longer afraid. Swimming into hemoglobin, "What should I learn from this?"

Gabriel says, "Do you hear that?"

Just then, a pop song plays inside her blood. "Watermelon sugar high, watermelon sugar high, watermelon sugar."

"What does this mean?" Rosa is so confused, bumping into white blood cells.

"You will know in time. Are you ready to leave your bloodline now?" Rosa declares, "Yes."

Standing back inside the cave, Rosa is trying to link the symbols, the sun, the moon, the stars, the tree of life, the all-seeing eye, the seed pod, the never-ending scrolls of paper, the blood, the watermelon seeds, and the sugar in her blood. "Gabriel, please help me."

"You are doing well, child. Much better than you realize.

Just then, Rosa senses a woman in the shadows. "Come closer, dear." The soft voice reaches out to Rosa. "Mother?" Rosa leaps to her side. Kneeling, Rosa's head falls to her mother's lap. Rosa weeps.

"Now, now, child. I am so proud of you. I love you so much. You have had this in you all the time."

Her mother soothes her soul and gently runs her fingers through her hair.

"Mother, how long has it been? It feels like forever since we have embraced." Rosa lifts her chin towards her mother's face.

"We are of the supreme council. Do you remember your crown?"

"My crown?" Rosa feels the electric buzz at the crown chakra of her head. Like bumble bees buzzing beside her ears, the vibration shivers quickly up and down her spine. With her mother's touch, like a unicorn growing a horn, Rosa's crown grows from the top of her head. Lusters of diamonds, brilliantly cut, line the height. The vault of Rosa's memory bank is now open. Rosa squeezes her bottom as tight as possible when she places her hands on both sides of her head and crown. Now in a seated position, the pressure, like a rocket blasting towards space, presses Rosa's bottom and feet deep into the bedrock beneath her. "Gabriel," Rosa screams out.

A white light banishes the darkness, and a portal opens above Rosa. The waters hang above her crown in the cave. Mother is gone now. The coronation is complete.

I have one more place to show you. Are you ready?"
Gabriel turns to Rosa as she replies. "Yes."

"Do you see the large body of water hovering above
us now?"

"Yes," replies Rosa.

"Good, we are going to step into the water now. The
portal is spawning. Follow me," says Gabriel.

Rosa looks down; the cave floor is now a sandy beach,
and thousands of glistening pearls are everywhere.

"Rosa," Gabriel says, "Here are the pearls of wisdom
you seek."

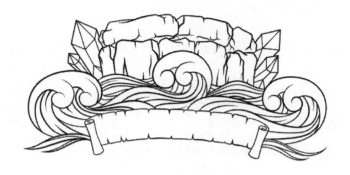

CHAPTER NINE

osa enters the salt water and walks on the seabed floor like a turtle hugging the ground, moving slowly and low. The soft sand squishes between her feet and toes. She can sense that her father is close by. "Father, are you there?"

"Yef, Rofa." He calls out to her. "Do not be afraid."

Rosa pushes past the giant kelp growing beside massive monolith stone pillars. The seaweed sways back and forth, lightly tickling her ankles.

"Thif if Atlantean," Father says.

Rosa starts to recall the temple on the mountain.

"I go by many namef, Rofa, and here waf my beavtifvl city. I fhared it with the God Pofeidon. Rofa, I called yovr people to Egypt before my great city flooded. The people were falling into irrational, mortal ignorance. The nation became fvll of wicked magicianf and, confeqvently, declared war. They had to experience a fpiritval involvtion. It waf the only way, the prereqvifite to the evolvtion of confciovfneff."

Feeling like a mermaid without a tail, Rosa touches her skin. The water is blueish green, with sparkles of sunlight breaking through the surface. The water feels dense, almost like oil. She is buoyant. Gliding through the water, she listens as closely as possible to her father's words; she is in awe of being underwater. Drowning in water is her greatest fear come to life, yet Rosa is one with the water. It feels like

Washington, D.C., strong and fortified. There are stone pillars, and the temple before her is massive.

"Afgard, my holy and facred movntain, Movnt Moriah, New Iervfalem. All pyramidf and templef pattern after thif great fanctvary. My citief of gold are in Egypt, Mexico, Cvba, and there are otherf in Central America. Before the deftrvction, my Initiate-Prieftf of the Sacred Feather, who promifed to retvrn to their miffionary fettlementf, never retvrned. Bvt for a felect few, I carried them to Egypt with the fecret teachingf. In Egypt, they eftablifhed learning centerf and promvlgated the code, clothed in the langvage of fymbolifm, too, af they deemed worthy to receive it. They tavght the fecretf."

"The hybrid hvman race if an old ftory, my dear, af I recall 560,000,000 yearf old. There have been memberf of the Atlantean covncil, both Syrian civilizationf and Annvnaki prefent. The magic waf dark. It took three floodf to bring balance and order to ovr people. The moleftation of technology cavfed fhiftf in the polef, global cooling, and ice agef. We divided, and the children fled. Twelve grovpf of civilization ftarted flowly—fome in Egypt, otherf on iflandf west of Africa (Canary Iflandf). The Mv gvarded the portal in the Pacific (Eafter Iflandf). More warf have broken ovt." Father retold.

Gaberial adds. "Father is the essence of time. The great pharaoh ate and buried the watermelon seeds with him, as eating watermelon assists him in maintaining his bloodline and procreating to strengthen his fertility."

"Yov recall the fymbolf well, my child. The alpha and beta carotene, the fvgar, reflectf in yovr eyef, Rofa. Yovr eye color refvltf from yovr DNA and yovr bloodline, child. Come clofer; I want yov to read the infcriptionf etched vnto the fovndational cornerftonef here in Atlantean." Father asks.

Rosa reaches out to read the stones. She pushes back the seaweed and reaches to touch the rocks. They turn to powder, a powder that resembles talc. "I don't understand, Father?"

"Keep reading it," he encourages her. The names of the stones are iron, chlorella, and spirulina.

"Father, this is all seaweed," proclaims Rosa.

"Thif if all medicine," proclaims Father.

He was right; everything that Archangel Gabriel had shown her was vitamins, symbols for medicine: Vitamin E Oil, Vitamin D, calcium, melatonin, watermelon, which converts to Vitamin A, and now there is kelp, iron, and other seaweeds.

"Come clofer, davghter; I will take yov to the heart of the city, to the fecret chamber, the vavlt."

Rosa follows her father. She senses it before she sees it.

Rosa enters the holy of holies in the heart of the Golden City, past the Golden Gate.

"Study clofely," Father whispers.

Rosa swims to a powerful, clear crystal. It grows from the seabed floor and feeds off the seaweed's minerals. Within a lightning flash, Rosa is inside the crystal.

It is like glass and sand, but the crystal has a message. In the fine print, a secret message typed: "KGB, KGB, KGB, etc...." Rosa feels frightened of these letters.

"Liften to the meffage, Rofa," her father whispers.

Like poison ink spelling out of a typewriter, she decrypts the message. A poison is leaking out of the crystal. Like ink spelling out, the poison is spreading out of the crystal. Sea eels swim under Rosa's feet. She leaps at her father. An eel flashed Rosa a pearly white grin. Father gently reaches down, grabs the eel behind its head, and instantly transforms it into a staff.

Rosa looks on with disbelief. "It's real. It's all real. All the stories and paintings." She knows in her heart. Deep down in her heart, she has always known that her father is real. That she, Rosa, is honest.

For some odd reason, Rosa knows the crystals represent her teeth. The pearls of wisdom represent her and everyone's teeth. The poisonous ink is mercury, the quicksilver amalgam used in fillings. These metals are leaking from her teeth and her people's teeth. The poisoning had happened before, during the time of the Atlanteans. They also experimented with adding metal to the teeth. The mercury was the core of the poison that turned the people wicked with headaches, tremors, difficulty sleeping, impaired sensations, muscle weakness, twitching, kidney damage, nervousness, and breathing difficulties. The crystals and teeth are now full of glass, not metal.

Rosa knew that since 1997 amalgam and mercury fillings had declined, and now white composite or porcelain filling material was being used and practiced. The people were healing. The institute talked about it. Something about the collective conscience. Crawl, he knew about it. They were speaking of healing the past, present, and future.

The antidotes: Vitamins K, Vitamin G, also known as Riboflavin and Vitamin B. It is all starting to dawn on Rosa. The hieroglyphs are chemical and chemistry medical prescriptions. The cave is full of medicines: powdered seaweed, liquid Vitamins K, G, and B. The vitamins and watermelon are all the secrets to longevity, youth, and vitality. The secrets of plant medicine are to keep humans healthy, open the heart, and the All-Seeing Eye. To purify heavy metals from the blood.

Rosa had heard of people doing heavy metal detox, but she had never stopped to think that the fillings in her mouth may be poisoning her. And what of the MRIs that Rosa had back in the States? Back in Charlottesville, at the University of Virginia. She remembered her teeth aching after the MRIs, the pain, and the depression. Three of her teeth had cracked. One even had to be pulled. All the teeth affected by the MRIs had mercury amalgam fillings. Rosa needs this medicine. Her headaches, Rosa thought. "Wait, my headaches started with the first MRI." The world needs this medicine. Rosa turns to thank her father, but he is gone.

Rosa does not feel afraid under the water.

Soon Archangel Gabriel returns. "Rosa, this is much information, and not all who hear will believe you. There will be those that scoff at you and laugh at you.

There will be those who will believe in your visions and those who will call you a quack, but I am giving you this feather to put in your cap. I am here to place a seal over what you have seen. Go now; you have received the message, and what you have seen and heard is correct. I declare it so, and I am a messenger of the Holy Lord God Almighty."

CHAPTER TEN

"Shhh," beckons Wailer. But it has been an hour since anyone has spoken. The lack of oxygen in the air, the darkness, and the confusion have kept the three soldiers in a trance. "Do you hear that?" Wailer whispers. "Is that music?"

At the top of a waterfall cascading down into a cement pool, the three warriors gaze into the cave's opening. In front of them lies a deep blue pool of water with about 200 yards of pristine, white sandy beach. Like a mini holiday resort, the beach has lounge chairs, umbrellas, and tiki bars. Shaking his head in disbelief, Wailer leaves Brass and Crawl to move closer to get facial identifications. Men dressed in civilian clothes with black military boots parade about the corners of the boardwalk with heavily armed assault rifles. Overhearing men speak of smuggling the subsequent shipments, the discovery hits Wailer like a tidal wave.

The Earth's makeup is 71 percent water, but only about 1.2 percent is drinking water. This water is the center of life, legends, and myths—the fountain of youth. The faces and location are all about the water here, not about drugs, the arms race, the land, the gold, or even the money.

Wailer flashes back to his mornings of Sabbath school and remembers the woman at the well in John 4: 13 – 14. Jesus told her, "Everyone who drinks this water will be thirsty again. But whoever drinks the water I give him will never thirst. Indeed, the water I give him will become in him a fount of water springing up to eternal life." The woman said to Him, "Sir, give me this water so that I will not get thirsty and have to keep coming here to draw water."

This underground spring contains the most precious, pristine element known to man, known to Earth. Knowing that he and his comrades are in hot water, Wailer maneuvers to return to Crawl and Brass, but spies are on guard. Immediately viewed as a breach, an alarm sounds off. Brass and Crawl watch from above. Seconds later, an explosion; the air is full of sulfur, and men are shouting and yelling.

CHAPTER ELEVEN

Explosions go off above Rosa's head. Red and yellow fire streams into the air as she watches through the water, suspended above her by the force field of the portal. "Gabriel," shouts Rosa. But Gabriel is gone. She stares at the cave paintings: all the pearls and the ocean waves. The ancient ruins of the broken city are dripping paint before her eyes. Rosa says a prayer, "Dear Father Time and Mother Earth, thank you for the secrets and the wisdom you have entrusted and shared with me. I promise to stay alive and carry your message as your high priestess of the Sacred Feather promised in Atlantean. Thank you for these pearls of wisdom. I love you, and now I know why you brought me here. Why I must go back home."

Gripped with adrenaline, Rosa crouches like a tigress toward the ground. As if landing on a magnetic field trampoline, Rosa launches and torpedoes herself into the hanging body of water. She swims to a tunnel opening. Entirely operating on human-machine conditioning, Rosa is alert to every sound. Again, Rosa hunches like a tigress in a damp cave opening. Peering out over the pool of water, she sees her comrades and feels relieved.

Spotting Crawl, Rosa begins to swim along the back side of the cave's edge.

"We have got to find a way out of here." Crawl snarls, "Give me your hand, Brass."

Slowly Brass makes her way down the slippery face of the cave and follows Crawl's lead.

Shots of gunfire ring out in the cave.

Wailer leaps from a rock's edge and dives into the pool of water.

Seeing Wailer jump into the dark water and sensing his distress, Rosa swims toward him. Knowing Rosa can take them to the underwater cave, knowing she can save her friends, Rosa swims. Her heart pounding, Rosa swims harder.

Keeping his eye on Wailer, Crawl dives into the water. Brass, within arm's reach, slips in behind Crawl. Within seconds, Wailer grips Crawl's hand. Crawl locks him close and pulls him down under the water. Bullets torpedo through the water, nearly penetrating Wailer's flesh. Within seconds Rosa clasps Crawl's hand and pulls him more profoundly under the water. He knows that Rosa is alive. This fuels his adrenaline. Crawl, Wailer, and Brass slip into the dark water following Rosa's lead. Four dark shadows break the surface. Circling above them, like hammerhead sharks, they dominate for speed toward Brass.

Falling from the water and landing in the open cave, Brass sees Rosa. With tears of joy, the sisters embrace.

"How?" Brass stutters.

"I don't have time to explain," states Rosa. Her green eyes bounced toward the massive body of water suspended above them. "We must move quickly," exclaims Rosa. Pointing to the cave paintings, she summons them to follow her. Back through the corridors, Rosa listens for the hum of direction, the vibration.

"Did you hear that?" hushes Wailer.

"They have broken through," states Rosa.

"Who are they, and why are they here?" Rosa gives them a troubled look.

"No time to explain," shouts Wailer.

"We must get out of here fast," chimes Brass.

Following Rosa's lead, the four wind back into the tunnels. Overjoyed and ecstatic to be in her presence, Crawl stays close to Rosa. Knowing he will never let his grip slip again.

Crawl felt it the moment he laid his eyes on her, the heat and the magic. It took everything in him to contain himself. Rosa teared up with joy and excitement at the Banana Rum pub. Crawl remembers how she took his hand. He could feel her heart beating, and when Rosa began to cry, her eyes filling with water, he could not help but tear up himself. It was not even about the treasure or the thrill of the chase. It had something to do with the way she trusted him, the way she grabbed his hand. He pushed his thoughts and emotions to the side, rationalizing his feelings. Nevertheless, now that Rosa is back in his grip, he can't stand the thought of losing her like that. With a firm squeeze, he pulls Rosa toward him. Rosa stops and turns to Crawl.

Crawl cups Rosa's face with his trusting hands. Brass and Wailer slip past the couple and for a split-second, time stops. Rosa beams up at Crawl, glowing. Losing himself in her emerald eyes, he moves his fingers across her lips. Rosa grips Crawl's muscular biceps to keep herself standing. Crawl senses how weak she is and pulls her close. Tightly, Rosa holds on to Crawl, but her body goes limp. She is weak in the knees and can barely stand in his presence.

Crawl whispers into Rosa's ear, "You are safe, kid. I have my eye on you." Crawl bends his thick neck like a swan, and his hot lips press against Rosa's soft mouth. Rosa's eyes gleam open. A spark ignites in her heart.

Sensing the men following are close by, Rosa grabs Crawl's hand, and like an unseen guide, instinctively, she leads him deeper into the belly of the stone maze. Moving beyond the pit, twelve tunnels and corridors open in different directions. Stopping at the hole, she shows Crawl the cuts on her legs from the serrated coral; she points out and explains how she fell through the seafloor.

"We can lose them here," exclaims Rosa to the gang. Running her hands along the cool, damp rock wall, she guides everyone by the sound of her heart pinging in her ears. Quickening her steps with the now constant hum, they slip into a dark tunnel. Like a human glow stick, she leads and lights the way.

"What's happening here, Sis," stammers Brass. "Are you glowing?"

"No," explains Rosa, "but the rocks glow when I touch the walls. The stones are alive with energy, and I am conducting the power into light. I am a semiconductor, I guess?"

The tunnel becomes narrower and begins to snake and weave up and down, deeper and deeper into the

Earth's crust. Stopping short of a plummeting ledge,
the hum in Rosa's ear magnifies to a roar.

CHAPTER TWELVE

A massive waterfall plummets a hundred yards away. Billowing hot steam rises from a bottomless pit, forming clouds above Rosa, Brass, Crawl, and Wailer. Parrots, humming-birds, butterflies, and fireflies fill the dense banana and palm canopies. An enormous tree as ancient as the Ancient of Days is in the middle. Moving toward the waterfall, Rosa begins to climb a slippery rock face. Again, pulling on vines, she lifts herself to a ledge.

Rosa senses a pulse at the top of the waterfall, like the beat of her heart. Turning her head like a dove, she peers into a large emerald green crystal stone the size of two full-grown men. Rosa reaches out her arms and places her hands on the rock.

Like a wave of water, the white light penetrates Rosa's fingertips and into her bloodstream—the light flowing into her veins and blood. The light beams through her arms, filling every fiber of her being. The light travels into her pounding breast. Like a dove in flight, Rosa's heart plumes and expands, and with an annihilating flash of white light, Rosa's feather heart bursts open with the call of the parrots.

CHAPTER THIRTEEN

Opening her eyes, Rosa peers up at the doctor. "Rosa, Rosa!" The doctor repeats himself. "Can you hear me?" he says, looking into her emerald eyes.

"Yes," whispers Rosa. "Where am I?"

"Instituto de Neurologia in Havana, Cuba," states the doctor. "I am so happy you are awake, my child."

Rosa glances at a newspaper on her side table. Headlines read, "Cuba Free of pandemic cholera and dysentery. Major earthquake disrupts underwater reservoir, cleansing Cuban drinking water of bacteria."

"Would you like a glass of water, Rosa? Are you thirsty," asks the doctor. "You have been in a fever-induced coma for 72 hours from the pandemic and the dysentery. You were very sick, my child. I have kept a close eye on you day and night. Would you like to sit up and maybe get some fresh air?" asks the man in the white lab coat.

Walking to the window, the doctor lifts open the glass window. The cool breeze fills the room and clears Rosa's head. Setting her bearings and touching her fingers to the back of her neck, Rosa softly requests, "Yes, I would like to have a glass of water."

Rolling the white sheets back, Rosa peers down at her legs. Pink scars, like the size of tiny shark teeth bites, dot her soft, supple bare legs.

The End.

Made in the USA
Middletown, DE
10 May 2024

54181857R00057